W9-BMV-429

Aani and the
TREE HUGGERS

by Jeannine Atkins • *illustrated by* Venantius J. Pinto

LEE & LOW BOOKS Inc.
New York

Text copyright © 1995 by Jeannine Atkins
Illustrations copyright © 1995 by Venantius J. Pinto
All rights reserved. No part of the contents of this book may be reproduced
by any means without the written permission of the publisher.
LEE & LOW BOOKS Inc., 95 Madison Avenue, New York, NY 10016
leeandlow.com

Manufactured in China by South China Printing Co., February 2013

Book design by Christy Hale
Book Production by The Kids at Our House

The text is set in Bernhard.
The illustrations are rendered in gouache on paper.

(HC) 10 9 8 7 6 5 4
(PB) 15 14 13 12 11 10 9

FIRST EDITION

Library of Congress Cataloging-in-Publication Data
Atkins, Jeannine.
Aani and the tree huggers/by Jeannine Atkins; illustrated by Venantius J. Pinto — 1st ed.
p. cm.
Summary: Based on true events in India in the 1970s, young Aani and the other women
in her village defend their forest from developers by wrapping their arms around
the trees, making it impossible to cut them down.
ISBN: 978-1-880000-24-3 (hc)   ISBN: 978-1-58430-004-5 (pb)
[1. Trees—Fiction. 2. Conservation of natural resources—Fiction. 3. India—Fiction.]
I. Pinto, Venantius J., ill. II. Title.
PZ7.A8634Aan   1995
[Fic]—dc20   95-2036   CIP   AC

To Pat Cook and Ed Smith—J.A.

For Anupama, Eurisca, Franciska, Joyce, Ketki, Mildred, Nadisha,
and Olayinka: creatively courageous women;
dreamers and shakers—V.J.P.

Aani set down the basket of brown nuts she'd been gathering and sat beneath her favorite tree. Every day, at least once, she leaned gratefully against its thick, rough trunk. Here she had daydreams too large to fit in her family's crowded hut where crying babies, her grandfather's complaints, and her sisters' gossip drowned out the sounds of her own thinking.

Aani crushed a red berry to make a red spot on her forehead like her mother's. She was weaving grass around her ankle, like the silver bracelets married women wore, when she heard rumbling and roaring. The sound was as angry as a tiger's growl. It was louder than the thunder that seemed like the stormy voice of the snow-capped mountains. Aani glanced at the Himalayas, but the noise was not coming from that snowy home of the spirits.

As the grinding and gnashing grew louder, Aani sprang up.
She knocked over her basket of nuts as she ran toward home.

Her mother was not in their hut or in the yard. Her father and the other men were in a distant field, cutting stalks of rice.

Aani ran to the river and found her mother filling a jug with water.

"Mother! Can you hear the noise?" Aani cried.

Her mother put down the jug and listened. A woman beside her stopped whisking the sari she was washing through the water. Several women, some with babies bouncing on their backs, rushed toward them.

Aani's mother looked past the smoke that curled between the tree trunks. "It's a truck," she told Aani. "A gigantic and swift cart."

The other women had reached them.

"It is as we heard from the forest runners," Kalawati said. Everyone turned to listen respectfully, since Kalawati was the oldest person in the village. "The men from the city have come to take the woods."

Aani's mother frowned. "But the forest has always been here. Our people have always been here."

"The men from the city will say that we don't own it. We don't have papers," Kalawati said. "That's what they told them in the other village."

The rumbling had stopped. Aani lifted the hem of her sari and ran toward the place that had just turned silent. She sped past the rice fields, where the men carried sheaves of rice on their backs, like golden capes. Aani's mother and the other women dropped their baskets and pots and hurried behind her. The silver bracelets on their wrists and ankles jangled.

They stopped when they saw the truck. Several men swung axes. One held a tool with jagged and sharp steel teeth.

"Namaste." Aani and the women put their hands together, prayerlike, and bowed their heads. The men continued to swing their silver axes at the bottoms of small trees. The metal first broke the bark. The gashes grew wider. One man pushed a broken tree. It thudded to the ground. Aani's mother covered her mouth.

"Stop!" Kalawati cried.

A man pulled the chain of a saw. The grinding noise was shrill,
but Kalawati spoke loudly. "The trees give us their fruit and berries.

Their wood provides our houses and our plows and hoes. The roots keep the land from sliding when the heavy winds and rain come off the mountains."

The men continued to swing axes. The swaying and buckling branches let Aani see the wind, and the wind let her see spirits. A man with an ax seemed only to touch a tree and it crashed down. Kalawati ran toward this man.

"Kalawati, stop!" the women called.

Kalawati grabbed for the man's ax. The man pushed Kalawati, and she tumbled.

"Get out of the way!" yelled the man.

"We use these branches for our fires," Kalawati said. "We need them to cook our food and warm our homes."

Another man waved a piece of paper. "We've got orders."

"Already you've cut more than we cut in a year," Kalawati said. "Animals live among these trees. Where can they go?"

Another man with an ax brushed past Kalawati. He walked by Aani's basket and nuts, close to the tree that Aani sat beneath every day. Aani ran toward him.

"Come back!" her mother called.

Aani threw her arms around the tree. She pressed herself against it. The man and his ax were at her back. How easily that ax had pierced the bark!

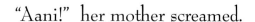

"Aani!" her mother screamed.

Aani heard her fear, but she pressed herself closer to the tree, close, so that nothing came between them. The bark scraped her cheek. She didn't look until the sounds of the saws and swinging axes stopped. The wind wound around the trees so that the leaves softly whoo-hooed and hummed. And then she saw that all around her, women and children were hugging trees.

The red tikas on the women's foreheads made bright spots in the
forest. The men had put down their axes and were whispering.

Then one of them said, "Please, go home."

"This is our home," said Kalawati.

"We will give you a thousand rupees just to leave," he replied.

Aani thought about what a thousand rupees might buy. A goat, so that they wouldn't have to carry kindling on their backs. It could buy new scythes for cutting rice, and enough tea and sugar to last everyone for years.

"No," Kalawati said. "We don't need a thousand rupees. We need the trees."

Once again, Aani and the women clasped their arms around the trees. Aani didn't move until she heard the rumble of the trucks, first loud, then fainter. Rustling leaves and rattling branches again filled the forest with their music.

Aani dropped her arms from the tree.
"Namaste."
Peace was what they wished for everyone who came and left.

"What did you think you were doing?" Aani's mother asked. "I was so afraid."

"I was afraid, too," Aani said.

Kalawati started dancing. Another woman bounced her baby. Overhead, birds flew from tree to tree. Someone began to chant. Aani looked up at the great range of mountains, and whispered a prayer to the goddess mother of the world. The trees were safe, now. Everyone was safe.

Author's Note

This story is based on real events in northern India in the 1970s. The women, part of a movement known as the *Chipko Andolan* ("Hug the Tree Movement") were victorious. Today, councils meet within most villages to decide how many trees can be cut without endangering the land and those who live there. And every spring, new trees are planted.

Illustrator's Note

These illustrations were inspired by 17th century styles of northern Indian miniature painting: Basholi, Bilaspur, Devgarh, Kangra, and Pahari. Indian miniature styles of this time—that is, before the influence of Western modes of painting and perspective—depicted human figures most often in profile. I drew from various aspects of each style to arrive at a comprehensive articulation of the *shakti* (energy) personified by the women of the Chipko Andolan and of the forests, which survive today in northern India because of the bravery of people like Aani.

The combination of *rekhen* (lines) and *bindu* (dot) on the text pages is a device similar to that used as a "runner" to contain Indian spiritual manuscripts. The *bindu* stands as a reminder of the inner witness contained in all of us. One of several symbols for the third eye, the *bindu* is also a window into one's innermost being—a space to always turn to when in need of an answer.